The Mixed-Up Wishing Well

Ⓧ

Marcia Vaughan
Illustrated by François Ruyer

Chapters

			Page
Chapter 1		Loads of Toads	3
Chapter 2		String Bean?	8
Chapter 3		Shiny or Slimy?	12
Chapter 4		Pains and Chains	16
Chapter 5		Wise and True	20

Chapter 1
Loads of Toads

Once upon a time, there was an old stone wishing well at the edge of a forest. Moss covered the old well's ears, so he couldn't hear very well. Cobwebs covered his old eyes, so he couldn't see very well. Still, the old well did his best to make every wish come true.

Early one morning, the old well was fast asleep when the sound of dancing feet woke him up. Splash! A coin dropped into the well, brushing some cobwebs from his sleepy eyes.

"What's that?" asked the old well. "Who's here so early in the day?"

Looking up, the well saw Greedy Gus. He had on his fancy dancing boots and he was whirling a young lady round and round.

"It's Shy Sarah," the old well said. "I like it when Shy Sarah comes along to visit. But what is she doing with Greedy Gus?"

"Will you stand here, Sarah, while I talk with the well?" Gus asked. He danced over to the well and said softly,

"Hey there, wishing well, listen to me.
I wish to marry Sarah; she's as rich as can be.
I wish to be the one with **loads of loot**.
Now marry us quickly, so I can scoot!"

"Did he wish to be the one with **toads in his boots**?" the old well asked. "What a funny wish. But whatever Greedy Gus wants, Greedy Gus will get."

The water in the old well whirled and swirled. Splash! The water washed over the sides of the well and all over Gus.

"Toads!" shouted Gus. He squirmed and fell down as toads jumped out of his boots.

"Serves him right," Shy Sarah said. "He liked my money more than he liked me."

Chapter 2

String Bean?

Later that morning, along came two more greedy people. One was Duke Chickenheart and the other one was his bossy wife, Prune Hilda.

"Yes, dear. Of course, dear," whispered the duke.

"And don't you forget about me being queen!" shouted Prune Hilda.

"But dear," the duke asked in a whisper, "what if the real king and queen see us? They'll know we want to take their places."

"Don't you want to be king?" asked Prune Hilda.

"Yes. Yes, I do," said the duke.

"And don't you want me to be queen?" Prune Hilda shouted.

"Yes. Yes, I do," the duke said.

"Then do it now, or I'll do it myself!" his bossy wife cried.

"Yes, dear. But would you hold my hand?" the duke asked.

Then Duke Chickenheart whispered to the well,

"Wishy, wishy, wishing well,
I have a wish I want to tell.
We wish to be the **king** and **queen**,
so do it quick, before we're seen!"

"What's that?" asked the wishing well. "Did he say **string bean**? I wonder why he wishes to be a string bean? People are so funny. But whatever the duke wants, the duke will get."

The water in the old well whirled and swirled. Splash! It washed over both Duke Chickenheart and Prune Hilda. When the water had fallen back into the well, it left behind two string beans.

Chapter 3
Shiny or Slimy?

By and by, the old wishing well heard munching.

"What yummy string beans," said Vain Jane. She tossed a coin into the well and looked at herself in the water. "I am very beautiful," she said. "But I could look better."

"Who's there?" the old well asked. "Oh, it's that Vain Jane again. Oh, the wishes she makes! What does she want this time?"

Vain Jane leaned over the edge of the well and shouted,

"Yoo-hoo, well, make me happy!
Grant my wish and make it snappy.
I want to be a real beauty.
Hurry up and do your duty.
Make my teeth **dazzling white**.
So my smile is big and bright!"

"Did she say to make her teeth **black as night**?" the old well asked.

13

Vain Jane wanted more so she shouted,

"My friends will cry loads of tears
when I have huge **jewels in my ears**.
Shiny hair would suit me fine!
I will look just so divine!"

"Did she say a **mule's ears**?" the old well asked.
"And why does she want **slimy hair**? That's the
oddest thing I've ever heard," said the old well.
"People are so funny! But whatever Vain Jane wants,
Vain Jane will get."

The water in the old well whirled and swirled.
Splash! It washed all over Vain Jane. Her teeth turned
black. Her hair grew slimy. Then mule's ears grew out
of her head.

"I can hardly wait to show everyone how beautiful
I look!" said Vain Jane as she rushed away.

Chapter 4
Pains and Chains

Not long after Vain Jane had rushed away, two men came out of the forest. One man was large and round. The other man was little and skinny.

"I'll hold the lamp," the round one said. "Grab-a-lot, you slide down the chain and bring up the coins."

"But Rob-a-lot," said the little, skinny man, "how can I climb back up and bring the bag of coins? Why don't you go down the well?"

"I can't do it myself, Grab-a-lot!" shouted the large, round man. "The chain is not strong enough for me. Just toss the bag up to me. I'll hold on to it while you climb out."

So skinny, little Grab-a-lot slid down the chain. He stood on a stone at the bottom and began to scoop up coins.

"How's it going, Grab-a-lot?" called Rob-a-lot. Grab-a-lot called back,

"This stone is very slippery.
And these coins are quite a strain.
Whatever I do down in this old well,
I don't wish to **end up in pain**."

"What did he say?" the old well asked. "He wishes to **end up in chains**? Why would he wish to end up in chains? People are so funny. But whatever Grab-a-lot wants, Grab-a-lot will get."

The water in the old well whirled and swirled. Splash! It washed over both of the men. When the water had fallen back into the well, both men were locked in big chains.

Chapter 5
Wise and True

Just then, a young lady came along. It was Shy Sarah again. Shy Sarah did not like talking to other people, but she always liked talking to the old wishing well. She often came and sat by the old well. Shy Sarah thought that the old wishing well liked it when she came to visit.

Shy Sarah knew that the old well couldn't hear
well or see well. But she knew that he tried his best.
People's wishes just didn't turn out the way they
wanted. When people made a wish, the old well gave
them the wrong thing. Or was it the right thing?

Shy Sarah went up to the old well and sat on the edge. Then she looked into the well and said,

"Wishing well, wishing well, I'm as sad as I can be.
Gus liked my money more than he liked me.
I want to marry someone kind and **wise and true**.
Wishing well, wishing well, what can I do?"

"What did she say?" the old well asked. "Someone kind and **wise like you**? Oh, my! Shy Sarah wants to marry me! And whatever Shy Sarah wants, Shy Sarah will get!"

The water in the old well whirled and swirled faster and faster. Then a great rush of water washed out over the well.

When the water had fallen away, the stone well was gone. A kind, wise and true young man was there, just as Shy Sarah had wished. "My name is Frank Goodfellow," the young man said.

From that day on, Shy Sarah and Frank Goodfellow
lived in an old stone house at the edge of the forest.
Moss covered the walls. Cobwebs covered the windows.
And Shy Sarah and Frank Goodfellow lived happily
ever after. All's well that ends well.

"Things are always changing along the river bank," says Vole to Fingermouse. "See that seed blowing in the wind. Look again and it will be . . .

. . . a dandelion nodding in the breeze.''

"See that egg sitting in the nest. Look again, and out will come . . .

". . . a duckling going for a swim."

"See that tadpole wriggling its tail. Look again and it will be . . .

. . . a frog croaking on a stone."

"See that acorn falling to the ground.
Look again and it will grow into . . .